a collection of stories

sand nigga

by
bula barua

AuthorHouse™
1663 Liberty Drive
Bloomington, IN 47403
www.authorhouse.com
Phone: 1-800-839-8640

First published by AuthorHouse 7/1/11

ISBN: 978-1-4634-1988-2 (hc)
ISBN: 978-1-4634-1989-9 (sc)
ISBN: 978-1-4634-1987-5 (e)
Library of Congress Control Number: 2011909540

Printed in the United States of America
This book is printed on acid-free paper.

"Believe nothing,

> *no matter where you read it,*

> *or who said it,*

> *no matter if I have said it,*

> *unless it agrees with your own reason*

> *and your own common sense."*

Siddhārtha Gautama Buddha

(563-483 B.C.)

for all the artists

Children whose bodies
are needlessly **poisoned**
with drugs ~

Citizens whose great minds
remain **asleep** and **apathetic**
to the truth ~

Artists whose beautiful spirits
dream and **create** beyond
what currently exists ~

Know that our future is bright.
We shall overcome.
Stand up.

Once Upon a Time . . .   *2*

. . . Epilogue   *149*

Bula 2011

1

Once Upon a Time . . .

on this holy crown,

i gift you with the scenic route

through my mind.

you need no Google Maps or GPS,

for your valiant guides shall be the mad poets

i found hiding

in a dark and empty corner

in the **City of Angels**.

have you ever given *everything* you had,

every single ounce of your being,

for the promise of

love?

have you ever felt your heart gleefully *dance*

at the mere *sight* of your lover's smile?

have you ever considered another to be

an *extension* of you,

like your arm or your leg,

so that if he wasn't doing well,

that meant you also weren't doing well,

and you'd give everything to see him happy again?

have you ever known without a single doubt,

  that you'd gladly sacrifice *anything*

    to see your lover be flourish,

  even if it meant...

letting him go?

have you ever fallen...

undeniably,

all-consumingly,

insanely,

passionately...

in love?

i have.

it was spring, back then.

i had never tasted love's sweet nectar before.

then, one day...
Rumi convinced me that without **The One** by my side,
i was incomplete.

so, i decided to find **Him**.

on a moonlit night,

i stood on my tiny balcony and summoned

The Goddess of Sovereignty.

she magically appeared before me.

regal, beautiful, warm, and strong...

she was a *deity* of the grandest proportions.

she smiled and offered me the burgundy drink

from her golden chalice.

i gratefully took a deep sip.

it tasted like the scent of jasmine

on a balmy night's breeze...

feminine and sweet.

i fell into an ecstatic trance.

He *appeared.*

the world became art.

i danced instead of walked.
i forgot how to cry.

overwhelmed by His kisses,
i composed heartfelt melodies of musical laughter.

i wrote poetry.

i painted Him in every light,
while He softly dreamt.

i was reborn.

then,

the clock struck midnight.

his chariot turned into a crusty pumpkin,
and he sped off into the darkness,
pulling the silver lining right out from underneath
my bare and trusting feet.

he never looked back.

i lost my balance.

i fell swiftly into a rabbit hole, thickly laden with
ancient souls whispering *meaningless* advice to me.

after 108 sacred days of falling, i landed upon
an upside-down pyramid made of *bittersweet* croissants
and *myrrh-scented memories.*

it was snowing in paris.

i was sound but no longer safe, for the protective
haze of ignorance had been lifted from my universe.
i could see more clearly than ever before.

i was awake.

love had restored my vision.
the fall had restored my memory.

i once again found

my own watery interpretation of *beauty* and *life*,

and the journey we have all taken before,

and choose to take again and again...

and again and again and again and again and
again and again and again and again and
again and again and again and again
and again and again and again
again and again and again and
again and again and again
again and again and again
and again and again and
again and again and
again and again
and again and
again and
then once
more

.

on this holy crown,

i humbly gift you with my chronicles...
the deepest parts of me,
as a mere dipping of my fingers
into the everlasting grail.

Goodbye
Acrylic on Rice Paper
Bula Barua, 2010

wo.man

she is PERFECT.

perfectly *flawed*.

she wears her

scars

PROUDLY,

for they tell the **stories** of her **past**.

she is ...

humble   passionate   truth   brave   peace
poetry   mother   free   generous   moon   dance
twilight   beauty   sky   energy   laughter   nurturing
grace   strong   art   wind   sensual   warmth   pure
gentle   divine   compassion   truth   hips   lips
evolution   wisdom   Venus   Aphrodite   Durga
warrior   child   Goddess   light   immaculate

&

s   p   a   c   e

.

she wields her beauty

like a great sword,

ready to pierce the hearts

of those who dare

tres.pass

on

her

i n . d e p e n d e n c e .

consider yourself forewarned.

she loves **hard**

and expects **no less** in return.

she is GROWTH.

see her.

admire her scabs of wisdom,

for her mistakes are proof that she is

REAL.

she is undefined,

bound to **no** label,

but full of

infinite   meaning

.

she is...

the *brightest* constellation,

the absolute *essence* of soul,

the profound poet's thinking,

the spoken truth *untold...*

the lotus that blooms in the muddy pond,

the red rose who grows from the urban concrete,

the dewy skin that glows with the morning sun,

the cosmic power and strength

he feels...

she has given *birth*
to the greatest healers
of the greatest generations,
with her *womb*.

she has arrived.
stand up.

PEOPLE:

let no man see her suffer for *his* sins,

for she is the chosen vessel

who gives him his very

LIFE

from beneath her navel.

see her.

in her divine perfection
is your beautiful reflection.

Anita
Acrylic on Rice Paper
Bula Barua, 2010

2

the dream

i have been searching for a

MAN,

whose only existence (thus far)

is in my

dreams.

in his strong arms,

i am

FREE.

i am

free to make mistakes, free to come and go,
free to express myself, free to grow,
free to explore, free to speak the forbidden,
free to know the truth, free to hide,
free to change my mind,
free to disagree,
free from judgment and consequence,
&
free to love him,
as i wish.

he grants me the power to be.

two.gether,

we

serve humanity ∞ nourish those in need

inspire growth ∞ challenge the *status quo*

consciously evolve

cuddle in movie theaters ∞ speak in futures

alternate leading, following, and walking side-by-side

protect the weak ∞ dance ∞ play ∞ spread beauty

laugh out loud ∞ stay awake ∞ love

travel the world ∞ plant flowers ∞ listen to opera

surf ∞ cook ∞ learn ∞ recycle ∞ help ∞ teach ∞ create

&

indulge in <u>massive</u> amounts of PDA.

don't hate. congratulate.

we don't text. we have tea.

magic =

the **height** of his goals, the baritone of his laughter,

the l e n g t h of his strides,

the sweat on his muscles, the scent of his exhale,

the brilliance of his mind, the massage in his fingers,

the tenderness in his embrace,

the confidence of his gait, the loyalty in his gaze,

his love for color, his thoughtful introspections,

his courage to STAND UP for his principles,

his compassion for humanity,

his **desire** & ability to help,

& his bedtime stories.

he carries the

WORLD

on his back,

with his head held high

&

finds his way back to me

ever.y.sing.le.night

.

we stay _on_

the

relation.**ship**

he is my

karma,

reward,

King,

lover,

&

best friend.

he is my

PROOF that god **does** exist.

his hands were made to sculpt me.

he was sculpted by the heavens for me.

to love him is so easy.

he is my sun.

i am his truth.

in my dreams,
he has awakened me.

(fyi, I've been sleeping 10 hours a night.)

he has crossed oceans of time to find me.

he is almost here.

when he arrives, i will say to him...

DUDE!!!

Where the *hell* have you been?!? What took you so long?!?
I summoned you when I was 15 years old!!!

Do I look like a **ripe plum** to you?!?

Do you know what I've been through?!? Do you have any idea how
much I've seen and done without you?!? OMG!!! We are soooo
behind!!!

Do you know how **OLD** I am? I am **34**!!!!!!!!!

Technically, we should date for at least 1 year before getting engaged.
That puts me at **35** when you pop the question!!!

Well, everyone knows it takes at least 1 year to plan a decent wedding.
That means I'll be **36** when we're walking down the aisle!!!

I don't want to make babies right away. I'd like to wait a year and live
like newlyweds before we're changing diapers!!! So, after that 1 year,
I'll be **37**!!!

Then, when we do finally decide to have babies, it's not like it happens
right away!!! Hello?!? It takes 9 months to bake a cake in the oven,
and that's *not* including the time it takes to fertilize the chef!!! Let's just
say your boys are great swimmers, we conceive in 3 months, and I pop
out a munchkin 9 months later.

That puts me at **38** with my very first child!!!!!!!!!!!!!!!!

AND
I
WANT
10
KIDS!!!

he will flash his dreamy smile,

take me into his strong arms,

and whisper softly into my ear...

"Darling, I'm ready when you are."

ဒ

art

We press our souls firmly to each other
in a *duet* of infinite passion.

The walls between us crumble.

Synchronized heartbeats spiritually signal one another,
through our divine artistry.

I am so taken.

Your melody moves me.

I inhale your profound rhythms,
and let your bass line guide me.

I pick up my pen.

Stories of written tranquility begin to *flow*.

You are the light that imagines me.

Together, we create an *oeuvre* of utopian dreams
from another time long, long ago.

And my soul pockets you.

4

god within

genesis 1:27
so god created man in his own *image*

definition of the word *image*
one that exactly resembles another; a replica; a copy

premise
we *are* god

alternative premise (if you just can't swallow the above)
god is *within* us; we are *of* god

questions

why do we feed god artery-clogging junk food
with high fructose corn syrup, excess saturated fats,
massive amounts of sodium and refined sugars,
and processed "byproducts" with mystery ingredients
and toxic preservatives?

how can we let god sleep on the streets with nothing to eat
and nothing to keep him warm at night?

why do we judge and punish god for her mistakes?
how can we throw god behind bars, without healing him first?
why do we enslave god and ask her to enslave others?

why do we touch god with music that encourages him to be a
gangsta, playa, thug, pimp, and thief... and then get shot 50
times in the ass? why do we lyrically degrade her into a
promiscuous ho, ghetto bizzle, bitch, and dime?

why don't we let god sleep in more often?

more questions

why do we ask god to kill innocents on foreign soil
in the name of patriotism, oil, blood, and green paper with
images of dead presidents on it, oppression, and slavery?

why do we force god to carry prejudices, which she didn't start?
why do we take away god's free will?

why does god have to pay taxes?

how did we convince god that he is nothing more than a meat
body of flesh and bone?

why do we bitch and moan about god's cellulite, muffin top,
receding hairline, gut, double chin and crow's feet?

why do we surround god with others who are negative and
critical of her?

why do we abuse god when he is a child, and rob him of
the right to play, laugh, learn, dream, and be safe?

how can we make god cry?

scenario

imagine an angel.

she is holy, divine, and pure. she is loyalty and strength.
she is all that is good. she acts only from a space of truth,
kindness, compassion, and love. she is so pristinely beautiful,
that it almost hurts to look into her eyes.

she glows. she is *peace*.

ask yourself

would you lay this woman down next to a man who insults her,
abuses her, and makes her cry? would you passively watch,
as her wings got torn off by those who wished to ridicule and
punish her? would you allow her to be hurt?

that woman is **you**.

god within. stand up.

Fairy
Acrylic on Canvas
Bula Barua, 2010

5

modern-day slavery

Part 1: The Future

I took a trip to the year **2035** in my sister's secret time machine. Los Angeles looked like a colorful version of **The Jetsons**.

In the skies, humans were flying around in neon-colored, energy-efficient **smart** cars. On the crowded streets, they were dressed in organic, loose-fitting fabrics, and high platform shoes. Everyone seemed so bright, fast, happy, and **aware**, with a certain swagga' I hadn't seen before.

I walked slowly through **Skid Row**, on a quest to find the public library. The air was brisk and smelled of freshly baked bread. The sky was turquoise, with no signs of smog. There were no bums and no trash. The buildings were clean and free of graffiti. Charming sidewalk cafes and fine art galleries stood on each block, and colorful tulips lined the sidewalks. Somewhere in the distance, a saxophone wailed a lively jazz melody. The city was so **aesthetic** and **soulful**!

I tried to blend in with the crowd, but my messy ponytail, beat-up Pumas, frayed jeans, and baby tee, with the infamous graphic blue and red **Obama** and **Yes We Can**, looked outdated, faded, and very bland. I was definitely getting looks of curiosity!

I found the library and walked inside. There were no visible metal detectors or personnel working. It seemed that books were borrowed on **The Honor System**.

I followed the signs to the **History** section and found exactly what I was looking for. It was a memoir, called **The Kaleidoscope** by **Eden**, a beautiful and revolutionary writer in her 20's. In her book, Eden wrote of her memories as a fetus, inside of her mother's womb, in the year **2012**.

I lovingly opened the heavy hemp cover and turned to the first page.

Part 2: Book of Eden

On Planet Earth, it was the year **2012**, and humans were still acting like damned slaves. Hence, from this point on, I shall refer to them as **The Slaves**.

My Mother found her **purpose** in educating The Slaves through her exquisite beauty and art. I heard everything from behind the protective walls of her warm belly. I listened to countless conversations, plans, dreams, realizations, and experiences.

As we all know, back then, earth was designed to **trap** The Slaves right where they stood. Sadly, The Slaves fell for it every single day.
The irony is that they *could* have been free a lot sooner. They just *chose* not to be.

The Slaves were controlled by the pharmaceutical companies, who kept them sick and addicted to their **moneymaking poisons**. They even poisoned their own babies at school, just because they *"acted up"* or *"became distracted,"* as children will often do. For example, they often gave their babies a poison called **Ritalin**, which was chemically identical to **cocaine** and just as addictive.

It's almost as if The Slaves believed they should be **unfeeling robots**.

They viewed any emotion as *sickness*. Thus, to be sad meant you needed to take an anti-depressant, as they called them. To be happy meant you were probably already on one. But, the poisons never cured a single person. They only destroyed the physical brain tissue and numbed The Slaves into a state of **manic apathy.**

I recall a story about a young girl who had broken up with her boyfriend and felt sad. Her mother promptly took her to a **headshrinker**. (Back then, they still called them *psychiatrists* and they were legally practicing their deadly quackery.)

The ignorant headshrinker prescribed the young girl a psychotropic drug. A few weeks later, the girl took her own life.

Suicide was one of the many insanity-creating side effects (in small print, of course) of those psychotropic drugs, but neither the mother nor the daughter thought to read the fine print on the bottle.

Those poisons always *caused* what they were *supposed* to cure. However, The Slaves ignored the data, and *chose* to believe the headshrinkers instead.

Pan-African slaves in the Pre-Civil War times were forced through physical and emotional torture to *"Do as you're told!"* and *"Don't talk back!"* In contrast, these Modern-Day Slaves had the freedom to learn the truth and challenge oppression, but they *chose* to ignore this precious right.

The Slaves were shackled at the ankles by the nicotine industry, who kept them sucking on **cancer sticks** and coming back for more.
The Slaves *knew* the devastating effects of cancer sticks on their bodies, but still continued to use them, thus putting money back into the pockets of those who oppressed them.

They were brainwashed into stillness by the media who **hypnotically** told them every day that the economy was bad, the environment was disintegrating, war was upon them, and people couldn't be trusted.
But, hey, they could always buy a bottle of **Belvedere** to alleviate their sorrows!

It was 2012, and The Slaves still *believed* they were in a recession, so they kept creating it for themselves. Had the media declared the recession over, The Slaves would have inevitably celebrated and created abundance for themselves a lot sooner.

However, the media (funded by Big Pharma) would never be so truthful, for **fear** was their top-selling national product. After all, it's much easier to *control* an **apathetic population** than an empowered one.

In truth, The Slaves shouldn't have needed the media to give them a reason to wake up, not with the powerful spirits and minds they had.
However, they were in such a state of unconsciousness that they could not even *begin* to conceive that anything they saw or heard was not truth, much less strategize on how to change their universe.

The Slaves were constantly smacked-down by **headshrinker pee-ons** (therapists) who told them *what* they needed, and *who* they really were inside, based on *no* real science, but a false premise that they were push-button, stimulus-response based *animals*, with no free will of their own.

The Slaves were so **owned**, that they had forgotten how to breathe slow, deep, and healing breaths into their body's most ancient chakras. Instead, they breathed short and shallow breaths of distraction and fear.

Some of The Slaves were so unfeeling and so dispassionate, that they turned a **blind eye** to their own brothers and sisters in need, and instead strived to be like those who persecuted them.

The Slaves partook in the planet's **STD Pool**, selfishly spreading horrifying diseases to each other, simply because they *refused* to honor their bodies and spirits with basic protection and common sense.
When a cure for disease was found, they sabotaged and hid it, sacrificing humanity for insurance dollars. They poisoned their bodies with infected meats and liquids, and processed foods with cancer-causing preservatives and pesticides. It was a bad situation, all in all.

Somehow, The Slaves had **forgotten** to **think** for themselves.
Instead, they believed everything they read and heard, without first experiencing it for themselves.

The trillion-dollar evil companies kept The Slaves **dumb and down** and they never thought to fight back. They just accepted their condition as truth and circumstance, and continued to measure wealth by the accumulation of physical possessions and **dirty** currency paper.

Then, everything changed...

Part 3: The Awakening

The Child came.

With His truths, The Slaves remembered. With His love, The Slaves believed.

With His magnificent presence, The Slaves finally **unplugged** themselves. It was such a day of truth, empowerment, justice, and light!

Together, The Slaves toppled and sentenced the greed-consumed, evil criminals and trillion-dollar corporations.

They eliminated welfare.

They used their technology to destroy the weapons of human destruction, which they had created and hidden before.

Most importantly, they replaced the faulty Band-Aids they had been living with for so long, with *actual* truth and healing.

When The Slaves **collectively** believed and agreed upon a new world; when they focused their energies and spirits on making it real; and when they adhered to the pledge they had taken…

Freedom manifested into reality, and humanity triumphed once again.

Part 4: The Child's Speech

Emancipate yourselves!

From this day forward, we shall not believe, unless we see it for ourselves!

We shall not make fear-based decisions!

We shall not poison our bodies and minds!

We shall not act from a space of anger, greed, or dishonesty!

We shall not be victims to circumstance!

From this day forward, we shall know that we are perfect, for we are all knowing!

We are *not* animals! We are **spiritual beings**, made in the image of **ultimate truth** and **absolute perfection**!

From this day forward, we pledge to:

- ∞ Share our knowledge and understanding with each other, so as to bring about change more quickly;

- ∞ Build strong bodies free from drugs and poisons, which weaken and reduce our ability to *live*;

- ∞ Create a government designed and run for *all* the people, not just *some* of the people;

- ∞ Develop our minds to their fullest potentials, so that we may stand tall in truth and knowledge;

- ∞ Think, act, and speak constructively and for the betterment of the world and mankind;

- ∞ Heal and protect our beautiful planet;

- ∞ See that every man, woman, and child becomes physically, mentally, and spiritually strong; and

- ∞ Love and uplift one another!

Never again shall we compromise our self-respect. Instead, we shall stand tall and firm in our integrity!

We shall not have anti-war rallies! Instead, we shall **march for peace**!

We shall not continue the ethnic and religious prejudices of our forefathers! Instead, we hereby end all racial, ethnic, and religious prejudices on this planet, forevermore!

From this moment on, we are free!

And so it was...

Part 4: The Beginning

With tears in my eyes, I took a deep breath and closed the beautiful book, when I suddenly noticed a gold, engraved inscription on its back cover:

For Mama.

I love you.

~ Eden

My heart fluttered.

Amorous
Acrylic on Rice Paper
Bula Barua, 2010

6

sand nigga

"I am fine with who you choose.
I will not push you or pull you.
Only, I ask one thing.
Do not marry a Muslim or Black."

~ Auntie X

Welcome to My World

I am 34 years old and without child. In my culture, this means my ovaries are rapidly turning into **prunes**.

My family is from India. I grew up in Indiana.

Everything about me was an accident, including my name. My mother meant to name me *Buelah*, a name she had read in an English novel, but accidentally mispronounced. Thus, my name became **Bula**, pronounced *Boo-luh*.

According to my mother's obstetrician, I was supposed to be a boy, but I accidentally came out with girl bits. Oops.

I was supposed to be a scholarly doctor, engineer or lawyer. However, when I was 3 years old, I told my mother I would be an **actress**. She was mortified.

I was taught to be soft-spoken, submissive, and obedient. I was instructed to make no noise, while washing and drying the dishes. I was never to slam a door, raise my voice, or question authority. I was taught to be graceful, meek, and obedient of my parents and their friends under all circumstances.

Basically, I was taught to be **invisible**. I did *not* comply.

Sometimes, I think the universe decided to play a joke on my parents and give them the **exact opposite** of what they hoped for in their firstborn.

My First Dance

In kindergarten, Mrs. Sabla asked me to show my classmates an Indian dance as part of **Show and Tell**. I was delighted to share!

I excitedly took my place at the front of the classroom. However, as soon as I stood up, put my hands on my waist, and started *shakin' what my Momma gave me*, the entire classroom burst into hysterical laughter.

I was perplexed.

I changed my dance pose.

More hysterical laughter.

Dejected, I sat down in my seat and felt tears *sting* my eyes.

Mrs. Sabla scolded my heartless classmates momentarily and we went on with our day, as usual. However, I could still hear muffled snickering, and I felt it was all directed towards me.

I was only 5 years old. That was the start of a very *tumultuous* childhood.

The Wonder Years

In the 1st grade, the boys chased me around the playground, while clapping their hands on and off their mouths and screaming, "Aye yi yi!" Apparently, they were trying to imitate **Native Americans**, whom they ignorantly called Indians.

In the 2nd grade, the boys chased me around the playground, while beating their chests like gorillas and grunting, "Boo-boo-boo-luh! Boo-boo-boo-luh!" Apparently, they thought they were from the **Planet of the Apes** and I was their predator.

By the 5th grade, I was always the last person to be chosen on the dodge ball team and ranked as the slowest runner in gym class. When winter came around, to my horror, I found myself stuck with a **potbelly** that jiggled like a bowl of Jell-O when I walked.

Well, being a creative individual, I decided to fake a cold so I could see Dr. Edwards (my pediatrician who looked just like Bill Cosby.) After all, he knew everything.

Towards the end of my appointment, when I asked Dr. Edwards the golden question, "Dr. Edwards? How do I lose weight?" he warmly smiled, patted the top of my head, and wisely told me to stop eating peanut butter, and the potbelly should be gone by spring.

It didn't work.

High School

In the summer before my sophomore year of high school, I decided it was time to change my life.

I ditched my glasses and bought contact lenses. I went to the orthodontist and bought a retainer to put my newly grown fang in check. I got a home perm and bought some designer shirts from the mall with my hard-earned babysitting money. To be honest, I also stole money from my sister's piggy bank, but denied it when she confronted me. (Sorry, Kid.)

On the first day of high school, I noticed the boys were staring at me. I felt so self-conscious! I went into the girl's bathroom to see if I had food in my teeth, but found nothing unusual. When I came out, a tall and lanky senior winked at me. I then realized what was happening...

Nobody recognized me! What's more, I had somehow become (gasp) pretty! The ugly duckling had grown into a swan!

Yessssss!!!

Soon thereafter, I developed my first **Official Boyfriend**. His name was Steve. He was handsome, sweet, kind, and gentlemanly. He was a basketball player.

He was Pan-African.

Of course, since I wasn't allowed to talk to boys over the phone or go out with them after school, our relationship was quite limited and very innocent.

I had to hide the entire affair from my parents, and even my little sister, who at the time was a chronic tattletale.

Consequently, our relationship consisted of holding hands, while walking down the hallways in between our class periods.

A few weeks after we started our lovely hallway ritual, I found a folded note wedged into the crack of my locker.

It read: **"Your a fuckin nigga lova you sand nigga."**

Huh?

Until then, I had experienced racism in various forms, but this was taking it to a whole new level. First of all, what the hell was a **sand nigga**? I had never heard that term before, and I had no idea what it meant!

I showed the note to my best friend, and she explained that it is a derogatory term, used to describe a person of Arab descent.

Um... **Newsflash: I'M NOT ARAB!!!!!!!!!!!!!!!!!!!!!!!!!!!!!!!!!**

But, I guess I *could* be...

Actually, I could be a variety of ethnicities. My look is very universal. I have almond-shaped eyes, caramel skin, and silky black hair. In fact, I'm often mistaken for being Mexican, Spanish, Venezuelan, African, Burmese, Portuguese, Italian, Puerto Rican, Native American, Salvadorian, Filipina, Greek, Bi-Racial with every combination you can possibly think of, and everything else *except* what I *really* am (Northeastern Indian.)

Still, to know that anyone would call me an offensive term, whether or not it was *technically* true, was rather annoying.

But, I wasn't the only one who was annoyed. Clearly, The Note-Dropper was too, because I (a certified **sand nigga**) **loved** a **Nigga**!

As for being a **nigga lova**, Steve and I had gone nowhere near **The L Word**. I was only 15 and we had practically just met! Talk about trying to rush a few innocent teenagers into a serious situation, way before they are ready!

Ironically, it was that fact that kept me from sharing the note with Steve. I would be *sooooo* embarrassed if he thought (OMG) I *loved* him!

Racism is Dumb

Unfortunately, it didn't end with The Notedropper. Throughout my life, I have also found that many South Asians tend to be racist against Pan-Africans. I'm not saying *all* are this narrow-minded, but if I had a quarter for every time an Auntie told me not to marry a *"black"* or *"Muslim,"* I'd have at least $5 to my name!

Strangely, the leftover effects of **Colonialism** and **British Oppression** still have many of us avoiding the sun, so we don't get **too dark**.

Allow me to break it down for you:

Dark = Unattractive

Fair = Beautiful

British Accent = Wealthy and Educated

Village = Unsophisticated or Backwards

Some of my South Asian girlfriends, who have darker skin call themselves **darkies**. These beautiful women speak so bitterly about how they wish they were not so dark-skinned, and how they don't feel attractive because of their complexion.

Yet, it isn't so difficult to understand where such self-loathing comes from. After all, if fair skin is our standard of beauty, then dark skin must be our standard of **ugly**, right?

Personally, I've heard Aunties exemplify this perfectly, with statements such as:

> "You know, her mother did not want her to marry him because he is so black. Now, look! Her daughter is so dark! Who will marry the poor girl when she grows up? This is why you should always obey your parents."

(Yes, they were being serious.)

Even South Asian matrimonial websites call this out in a very blatant way, where complexion is an *attribute* by which to filter potential life partners. Sadly, few users on these sites dare to advertise themselves as being *dark*. Instead, they check the **wheatish** box.

But, here's the ironic part....

In the USA, even the **fairest** of South Asians are still considered to be **minorities**, just like Pan-Africans! In other words, the government doesn't see us as being that different from one another. In their eyes, brown equals brown.

Moreover, the **equal opportunity benefits**, such as scholarships, jobs, and educational grants, received in the USA for being a minority, exist largely as a *result* of the battles Pan-Africans fought in this country, long before our families even immigrated here. We reap the benefits of *their* victories, while *hating* the victors themselves!

Are we really this desperate to be part of a perceived winning group, who were at one time our oppressors? Seriously?

Or perhaps Africans remind us of our times as impoverished servants, picking **tea-leaves** in the hot sun, as our skin gradually turned **cocoa**...

Racism is Really, Really Dumb

A former college professor of mine once tried to explain to me that racism is a *"natural"* part of the South Asian social system of hierarchy. According to her, we South Asians consider ourselves to be inferior to white folk, so we think it's our right to treat Pan-Africans as inferior to us.

(Clearly, it's also our right to invent **weird** theories to justify the harmful, irrational, and destructive actions we take against mankind.)

Some of my South Asian friends speak factually about the animosity they have experienced from Pan-Africans in lower-income areas of urban America. Such animosity continually motivates their communities to engage in reverse-racism back towards their darker-skinned oppressors.

But when does the cycle of hatred, based on one's skin color end???

How can it *ever* end, as long as we keep denying our own responsibility and carrying its burdens forth, thus continuing its ugly traditions into the generations of our future?

Sadly, we only **decay in isolation**, as we deprive ourselves of the rich experiences this world and its people have to offer.

This world is way too small, and word of mouth is way too powerful for racism to exist anymore!

CITIZENS,

We must **think higher** & **be better**,

not just for ourselves, but for our children.

We are so much **MORE** than:

the color of our skin, the first soil we touch, a flag, a habit,

a belief, a blood type, a resume, a gender, a prejudice,

a war, a salary, a name, a birth certificate,

our BLOODY history...

We are **the answer**, **the future**, and **the cure**!

We are humanity!

Stand Up.

Courage
Acrylic on Japanese Rice Paper
Bula Barua, 2010

अ

afghan refugee

the dirt on her face is thick.

tear-tracks streak thickly down her gaunt cheeks.

the grime under her nails is dark.

her knees and knuckles are caked with dried blood.

her teeth are stained yellow and crooked.

and…

her eyelashes are like harp strings
that play a beautiful symphony
every
time
she
blinks.

she sits on a rock and begins to write.

Dear Mr. President,

Ask me again, *"What do you want to do for a living?"* Call me *"unstable"* and judge me once more. It matters not, for I finally know the truth.

I don't want to *do* for a living. I want to **BE** for a living.

I want to be **the light**, which inspires us to grow, breathe, rejoice, work, and love. I want to be **the hope** for the child whom you label as sick, but who sees the world more clearly than you do. I want to be **life**, **clarity**, **passion**, and the undeniable **voice** of courage.

I don't want to be your pill. I want to be **the cure**, which strengthens the immune system. I want to be clean drinking **water**, thick **books**, and nourishing **food** for my sisters and brothers.

I don't want to be your superstitions. I want to be **the truth**, which most people avoid.

I want to be **the answer** mankind has been searching for.

When your bombs destroyed my home, so did I destroy my faith in you.

When the power went out in my village, God reminded you of the promises you made to me, and the need for your presence here. But, you didn't hear him. You just **blamed** me.

On that day, I lost my trust in your ability to protect, provide for, fight for, respect, and cherish me my family. My trust was the tiny piece of **dental floss**, from which I hung on to your every promise.

Don't you see?

You were my rock, my goal, and my very hope that things would change for the better.

But, you **disappeared**.

When you left, I decided that the void you left behind would be filled with something newer, stronger, and whole-heartedly committed to seeing our day of peace and justice arrive.

On that day, I lost my trust in you, but I regained my trust in **me**.

Now, Mr. President…

Watch me in awe, as I study, learn, grow, and work to rebuild my country with my own bare hands, one heavy brick at a time.

And I shall succeed.

Fatima - age 15
(Kabul, Afghanistan)

Pearls
Acrylic on Rice Paper
Bula Barua, 2010

8

sari-draping 101

my girlfriend parvati comes over to borrow a **sari** to wear at her friend's wedding. thankfully, i have many pretty saris for her to choose from.

she selects an embroidered, blue, chiffon number. she puts on the jeweled blouse and cotton petticoat. we carefully tuck in the first part of the long chiffon fabric into the waistband of the petticoat.

confusion strikes. *how does mom do this part again?*

we experiment with a few different methods.

first, we try pleating the front. she looks like she is wearing a big, uneven potato sack.

next, we try wrapping it tightly and pinning it every few inches. she can't walk properly and looks like a waddling penguin.

finally, we pull the petticoat lower to accentuate her slim waist and curvy hips. she accidentally steps on it and the whole thing falls off.

in short, the lovely sari is 6 yards of *pure disaster*.

we go to www.youtube.com and search for *"how to put on a sari."* we find a video called, **tracy's guide to putting on a sari.** tracy is a buxom blonde woman from texas with a heavy, southern accent and a big, white smile.

we watch the video very carefully, pausing every few seconds to replicate exactly what tracy is doing.

our commentary:

> **parvati:** "man! she may not be indian, but she's got the indian stomach!"
>
> **me:** "how did she learn to do this?"
>
> **parvati:** "who cares! look how simple she makes it! easy-peezy!"

after several attempts, we finally manage to wrap the sari successfully, but it still doesn't look as refined as it should.

my mother would appreciate the effort, but would probably laugh hysterically at the video, and then be **horrified** that i couldn't just drape the sari in 5 minutes, like she taught me years ago.

in the end, we decide the safest solution is for her to go into the women's bathroom on the morning of the wedding. inevitably, there will be numerous aunties present, furiously primping and pinning their own saris. parvati will dramatically fumble and then ask an auntie for help with her sari.

there. problem solved.

except...

what happens when we are the aunties, and our daughters need help putting on their saris?

culture lives and dies with those who pass it down.

to pass it down unfiltered is nearly impossible, for we were raised in a foreign land.

does this mean our culture, heritage, and beautiful traditions will go with our parents?

should we even care?

9

tech.know.log.y

They Say:

Technology has evolved, so as to make the world a smaller place and our lives more efficient. It is intended to *supplement* humanity and bridge the gaps that physical distance creates.

I Feel:

Technology has allowed us to *detach* from each other, as we *substitute* artificial machinery and online interactions for true human interaction.

Are the 600 friends on your Facebook list truly your friends?

We have let technology *dehumanize* our existence. As a result, we are growingly *unaffected* by cruelty, sadness, and violence within our own communities and abroad.

What's more, we have already begun to stop celebrating the very thing that defines us: **Our Humanity**. Instead, we *sacrificially* offer it up to the machines we create and worship every day.

Personal Experiment:

I shall embark on a quiet revolution, in an effort to reconnect with myself by reconnecting with you.

I yearn to have a cup of chai with you in the same room, rather than texting entire conversations back and forth. I want to visit your home for dinner... *without* calling first.

Thus, for 1 whole week, I shall not text, use Facebook or Twitter, and shall limit cell phone usage to 2 minutes per conversation. Furthermore, when engaged in a face-to-face conversation, I shall put my phone in my purse and out of sight. I will no longer be "on call" for the whole world.

I'm doing this because I want to know if the feeling of interconnectedness technology provides me with is truly *authentic*, or if it is just an illusion.

However, before I can begin this experiment, I must first notify my friends of my decision to do this.

Let's start with Twitter. By the way, I am driving right now, but I can use my knees to steer.

(Typin' on ma crackberry in heavy LA traffic)

@meatballsngravy: hey hun i kant txt u nymor bc ma thumbs hurt waaa 2 much! but ur ma fav! woo hoo! fist pumpssss!

@bigpoppafriedchicken: hey hun! u txtn aint sexy cuz u b lookin lik a baby t-rex all up on ur crackberry! smh.

@anidapahty: pl stop sextin me. i'm not tryna c ur bits. putda shi awa. kthxbye.

@beatdatwittaboytoy: hey hun! lmao! no more txt 4 me! ma fingas r maaaad akin! neeta get ma ibrows dun agin! chubacca is chilaxn o ma forhead!

@contactlist: dizzammm! my parlel pkg skills r so impeccable its sexy! xoxoxo

10

his voice

I speak.

You **refuse** to hear me, but I continue to speak.

Don't you see?

A lover being silent is

blasphemous!

I **refuse** to be silenced by your **ego** & **rage**.
I will transcend your pride.

I AM A
MAN.

I cannot let my **wo**-man

be a better **man** than me.

I will fight until my death to protect something I love!

I am *not* a coward!

I don't hide from my demons.
I **stomp on** my demons!
I smoke my demons in the ass!

I am a <u>man</u>.
I right my wrongs!

I speak.

My words have been trying so hard
to reach you, that they have

S   T   R   E   T   C   H

marks.

I shall conquer my fears. I shall overcome every obstacle and cross over any line.

Make no mistake. You are not my first. I have engaged in this warfare before.

Yes, it is true that I have never experienced this much resistance before. You have built up your barriers to keep me away. You refuse to hear what I have to say. You put up your defenses and raise them higher and higher, with every advance I make.

Still, I began this battle, and I will win this war, for I am a romantic warrior fighting for the love of my life. I will *not* allow you to deprive me of the chance to fulfill my promises to you.

I will *not* give up. I will stay and fight until the end.

I speak.

You refuse to hear me, but guess what?

I will <u>not</u> back down.

I will continue to speak.

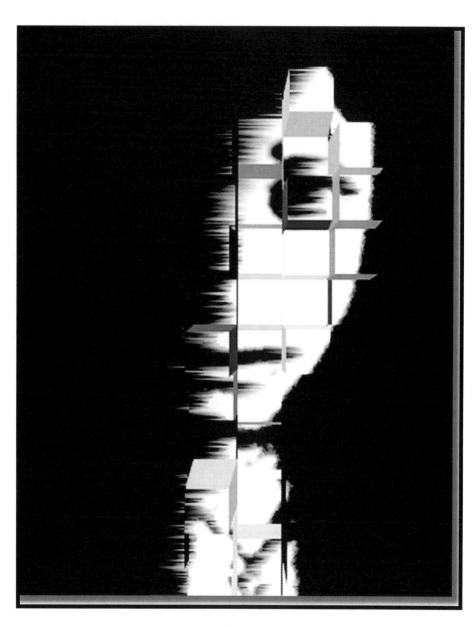

Clarity
Charcoal on Canvas
Bula Barua, 2011

creation

In the darkness of your shadow,
my vision was so confused.

I detached myself from all that was truth.

I abandoned reality, along with the very *essence* of me.

I was swallowed by your *false illusion* of safety.

As a candidate for your love, I became a political prisoner.

Then it got interesting…

We danced the Lambada of *deliberate* death.

Beautiful flames engulfed the chaotic Sinfonía.

You were the external force who monopolized me.

I justified your destruction as *common*, thinking I could just *remake* me… *later.*

I was naïve.

Freedom for me was in purification, as I became *separate* from the concept of *me with you*.

I disengaged, found energetic isolation and regained my own perception.

I grew so tall and wide, and threw my anchors far out to the sides. I knew right then I would be all right.

Look me up in the next lifetime...

12

signs

she sat alone in a larchmont coffee shop, sipping on an extra-hot chai latte with 12 swirls of whipped cream.

she looked up and suddenly noticed a large sign above the glass double doors, which led outside to the patio.

EXIT

**These doors are to remain
open at all times,
when building is occupied.**

she was struck by how *profound* and *poetic* the words were. in a world designed to keep its people trapped, rather than granting them true freedom, the coffee shop's sign seemed so unusual.

she thought back to the signs she saw on a daily basis. most of them were warnings about what she was *not* allowed to do.

**No Parking, No Crossing, No Loitering,
No Running, Do Not Enter, No Trespassing,
No Food or Drink, No U Turn, No Service,
No Cell Phones, No Speeding**

yet, this sign granted her true freedom.

she could go in and out as much as she wanted, so as to alternate between the lovely scenery outside, and the relaxing ambience indoors.

suddenly, it dawned on her...

she had crafted their relationship to be like the signs she saw everyday - inhibitive!

she had focused all her energy on creating guidelines for what she considered to be *unacceptable* behavior.

in the end, she had *suffocated* him with her fear-based restrictions.

but he needed her heart to be like the exit sign!

she began to write...

My Love,

I received a sign. Come and go as you please. My heart is always wide open, with no secrets, no inaccessible areas of darkness, and no hidden traps.

With me, you are free to explore, express, create, and play as you wish.

There is no judgment, no denial, and no limitations to what you may experience.

With time, I know you will cultivate a deep love, honor, and respect for my beloved heart, for you are safe here, with me.

Always.

Jules
Acrylic on Rice Paper
Bula Barua, 2010

13

cerchio

We stand

at the beginning of a *Locus* of all *Points*.

You are my Heart.

We form her *Diameter,*

standing *Equidistant* from her great core.

We move towards

each other, along a *Curved* line.

We create the *Circumference*

of a secret much greater than us.

Finally, we meet at *Zero.*

LOVE.

We walk together,
along the same *Curved* line.
STOP.

You turn. You walk away.
FROZEN.

You keep walking forward,
step by step, further away from me,
along a new *Perimeter.*

I smile.

We shall meet again
a *Thousand Times,*
My Love.

He Sees Me
Acrylic on Canvas
Cerchio, 2010

14

unsent letters

Dear Auntie X,

You can *choose* to be racist against African Americans and Muslims, if you'd like, for that is your prerogative. I still love you.

However, when I was 15 years old and I received that note wedged in my locker, I *chose* to take my focus *off* the color of a man's skin, and instead focus on the *content of his character*. I *chose* to believe in the dreams of Martin Luther King Jr. and live by the great words of Mahatma Gandhi.

Today, I *choose* to surround myself with those who treat me with love, respect and kindness; who share in the same goals and purposes as I do; who provide me with a safe space to communicate easily and freely about anything and everything; who challenge and encourage me to be a better human being; and who love, accept and celebrate me unconditionally.

With Love,

~ Sand Nigga

Dear The One,

I thought I met You so many times before, only to realize they were merely *Almosts*. Never one to settle, I simply refused to give up until I had the real *You* in my arms.

Then, May flowers bloomed and You finally found me! How gorgeous our time together was! I miss those days in your tiny apartment above the bustling city...

I painted so many *dreamscapes* while You slept. I dreamt so many *Happily Ever Afters*, while You worked. You were my beautiful everything... my teacher, my best friend, my lover, and my greatest inspiration.

Sadly, I learned that love alone isn't enough, not without dedication, effort, and courage. All those times I left, I never really meant it. I was just scared.

I only wish You knew how much I loved You. I always have.
I always will.

Dear Ex-Boyfriend,

(You know who you are)

When your car stalled, so did my trust. When the *Check Engine* light came on, it illuminated my doubts. You said I was safe with you, but **you lied**.

Funny thing is, I was never afraid of your lies. I was only afraid of the truths *behind* them.

When your engine refused to start, I got out of your car and walked to place where the ocean meets the sand. I got down on my knees and stared at the water's reflection.

A Goddess stared back at me and said,

> *"I don't know who you are, but I am Amazing!"*

Funny, how we lose perspective, sometimes.

Thank you,

~ Fatima

Dear New Man in Her Life,

That beautiful lady you're holding right now... she used to be mine.

You know those kisses she gives you every morning? She learned that from me. And you know how she holds you so tight, while she sleeps at night? She used to hold me that way, too. See, I'm the one who taught her how to love a man. I was her very first man.

I had her giving me all the love and affection she had inside of her. Every day, she'd laugh and cook and wait on me, hand and foot. But, she was too beautiful and I was too scared. I couldn't let her know how great she was or she would've left me for a better man!

So, I made her hide. I criticized her and put her down. I made her think she was worthless, so she'd be grateful to have me and *never* leave my side.

That beautiful lady you're holding right now... she used to be mine, until I taught her how to cry. In the end, I taught her how to say goodbye.

- Her Ex

(BTW, I'm stronger than you, and I have a faster car.)

Dear World,

Ever notice how children fight and make up so quickly? They say, *"I'm sorry"* and 5 minutes later, they're happily playing again! It's so simple!

They don't hold a grudge or bring it up later. They don't over-analyze. They don't stay stuck in the past. They simply accept kindness and move on.

What happens to us as we get older, that we makes us so jaded? Why's it so hard to wipe a slate totally clean? Why do we demand total perfection? Why's it so hard to weather the storms with love?

Imagine being with another who accepts you just as you are, never blames you, assumes the best, trusts you, and loves you unconditionally. What an incredible gift that would be, right?

Well, that's what I want. I want to **be** that for the whole world, and I want the whole world to be that for me. Judgment has no place in my life anymore.

The past doesn't matter. Every day is a blessed new chance.

Dear Mr. Bum,

I don't look you in the eyes, 'cuz I feel so guilty that you're starving, homeless and sad. I think I'm also kinda' scared, cuz if our eyes meet, I may feel your pain.

See, I'm a pretty happy person and I prefer to stay upbeat! So, I've learned to adjust my vision so you fade into the background when I walk by. This way, I hardly notice you at all!!!

Now, that doesn't mean you aren't important to me. You *totally* are! You definitely add to the scenery. Why, if you weren't around, the street wouldn't have nearly as much character! You add to the visual experience, for sure!!! :-)

Lately, I've noticed you have your own style. I guess that means you have a personality too, huh? Do you have dreams? How'd you end up like this? Oh, wait!!! Don't tell me, cuz it might depress me. I did wonder for a second, but I'm really better off not knowing.

Alrighty, then! Back to work now! You have a great day, Mr. Bum!

Tootles!
:-P

Dear Baby Girls,

There is no need to live a life of silent desperation. **Dream BIG!** Take up as much space as you need. Take up as much space as you *want*!

The waters may get rocky, but there are always safe ports in the storm. Follow the brightest star and the song in your heart, and you shall soon find them.

Never compromise your integrity. Keep your word and strive to reach your goals.

Know that you are beautiful, for you are **REAL**! You were never meant to compete with the bobble-headed, airbrushed insecurities you see in the checkout line. You are so much *more* than your skinny jeans and stiletto heels!

Learn to love yourself and honor your needs. Eat well. Exercise. Don't do drugs. You're no good to anyone if you're depleted, so you stay strong!

Sex does NOT equal love. Be the **hunter**, not the prey! You are *not* disposable. You are not an option. You are **priceless** and cannot be bought or sold!

You are the future!

Surround yourself with people who truly love you, not just tolerate you but **celebrate** you!

Remember that there is no such thing as failure. There are only challenges, which are really hidden opportunities to grow.

Never doubt that you are a fountain of courage. Never lose your hope. There is *always* a solution, and you will find it, for you have the ability to create absolutely anything you want!

Always trust in yourself, and know that you will be ok.
You are magnificent.

Dear American Customer,

I am not Chinese, Japanese, or Korean. **I am from Vietnam**.

Vietnam is a country in Southeast Asia. Our capital is Hanoi. My country is beautiful, with gorgeous plateaus, lagoons, and white-sand beaches.

Back home, I never washed dishes, did laundry, or cooked. We had servants who did all those things for us. Life was very easy, but because it is a Socialist country, we didn't have the same opportunities you do here. So, I made a very difficult choice and came to America. That was 10 years ago.

When I first arrived in Los Angeles, I wasn't prepared for how hard life would be here. I couldn't speak English, so nobody understood what I said. I had very little money, and my language barrier made it impossible for me to get a respectable office job.

At first, I stayed with my uncle and aunt. They owned a small nail salon. It was good business for them, because to do nails, you don't have to speak perfect English. You just have to be talented, like an **artist**.

I needed money, so I quickly learned how to do nails, got my license, and started working in their salon. Soon, I got married, moved out, and had a baby girl. Since then, I've learned basic English phrases, so I can talk with you. However, because of my accent, you can't understand me so easily. Still, I keep trying.

In my culture, we **never** touch people's feet. Feet are considered to be dirty. But, if you and I are friends, then I'm doing something nice for my friend, rather than being a slave, right? So, when you come in to get your mani and pedi, I try to talk to you, because it's my way of trying to be your friend.

Life can be so awkward.

But, when I see my daughter wearing nice American clothes and going to a good American school, I remember once again why I struggle so hard, and it's all worth it.

We are not so different, you and I. We may look differently and speak differently, but we are both just trying to survive and doing the best we can.

I see the beauty in you.

Please, American Customer, see the beauty in me too.

Dear Parking Ticket Enforcer,

You really pissed me off yesterday! I was parked in that spot for 3 extra minutes and the meter was **broken**! Still, you insisted on leaving me an early Christmas present, worth $60.

I've often wondered to myself what you look like, act like, and feel like inside, knowing that your job makes you one of the most despised people on planet earth. So, I decided to spy on you!

This morning, I sat in the Coffee Bean right next to a window, with a perfect view of my car, parked at the same broken meter. You pulled up in a wussy-looking golf cart, stepped outside, pulled out your pink notepad, and started to write.

I ran across the street to confront you, once and for all!

> **Me:** *"Hey! Why are you ticketing me for a broken meter?"*

> **You:** *"Maam, you can't park at a broken meter in LA."*

> **Me:** *"Where is that written? There is no sign!"*

> **You:** *"Maam, it's a law. Sorry, but you are getting this ticket."*

Frustration set in and I could no longer hold my tongue.

Me: *"Why do you do this job? Do you have any idea how awful you make people feel?"*

You: *"Maam, I hate my job, but I do it cuz I can't afford to work for minimum wage. I have a family to feed, and this job pays enough. It may seem like I'm doing something bad, but when you park over the limit, you're taking away a spot from someone else. So, I'm helping them out. That's what I tell myself every day."*

I was **stunned**. See, I had made you out to be this huge, despicable, ignorant, evil monster, but you are just a **man**. Your explanation didn't make sense to me. Yet, I didn't bother arguing, because I saw in your eyes a desperate, vulnerable, and helpless sincerity.

I know I didn't really say much in response, but I guess it's because my belief was totally deconstructed, which then made me wonder how many other **assumptions** I have wrong.

Dear Bollywood Family,

This morning, I got out of bed, brushed, flossed, showered, and came upstairs for breakfast. We shared a bright and cheery meal together. And of course, you just *had* to go there. Again.

Ugh.

As usual, as soon as the chai was poured, you started nagging me about **getting married** and **having babies**.

I've realized that it really doesn't matter what I accomplish. I could win *The Pulitzer*! I could win *American Idol* and the *Nobel Peace Prize*! I could receive an *Oscar* and then become the next *President* of *the World!* I could even become a *gazillionaire* and selflessly donate my money to end world famine, breast cancer and war.

Yet, even if I accomplished all that, you'd still consider my life's achievements to be substandard until I got married and had babies!

Well, I've figured out what's really going on here. Ever since we got those **12 Bollywood TV Channels**, which you guys watch all day, the nagging has been even louder! I think those dramatic soaps are to blame for my troubles.

It's time to call Dish Network.

15

confessions

uninvited guest

i hate when i create the agenda, invite my guests,
order the appetizers, and pick out the perfect little
black dress and heels...

only to mess it all up, just because i've got other
plans. baah!

she ≠ me

spent 34 years trying to change me from:

an artist to a scientist, bold to conservative, serene to fearful,
self-determined to obedient, friendly to cautious, rebellious to conforming,
single to married, brave to god-fearing, carefree to controlled,
ambitious to limited, thin to plump, competent to dependent,
talkative to quiet, confident to insecure, infinite to caged, &
me to her.

i spent 34 years resisting, until i realized...
only that which you resist can truly harm you.

today, i celebrate **me**.

persistence

some people put up walls
just to see if you care enough
to break them down.

secret

in the silence of the night,
i have often wished for just a *few* of your words,
rather than the thunderous applause
of a million people.

fear sucks

when i went into love with *fear*, believing i would fail, i sabotaged us, and thus created a self-fulfilling prophecy.

when i went into love with *excitement*, jumping in head-first and giving it all i had, i always came out victorious. whether we stayed together or not, i had the luxury of knowing i tried my very best, and didn't run away before we had a chance to begin.

i love the journey. no regrets.

choices

i once heard this rumor that a woman must *choose* between a lover and life-partner, for it's impossible to find both in the same man. well, i would like to make it known that this is an absolute lie.

we can have it all.

i believe

in life, we are either cause or effect.
your choice.

powder

powder sees a deer get shot in the woods.

crying, he places his hands on the animal's body
and pushes his life-force into him, so as to heal the
precious animal.

in the energy exchange, powder absorbs the deer's
pain and almost dies.

powder must learn how to push his light out,
without absorbing the darkness around him.

maybe that's what it's all about...

Punjabi Princess
Acrylic on Rice Paper
Bula Barua, 2010

• • •
Epilogue

Time passed slowly at first, but soon picked up Her pace.

Glorious suns migrated from the west to the east, and the Pale Moon eclipsed with Mother Earth.

Spring reluctantly left, only to return to my arms once again.

I gazed at the dark, Floridian night sky with a lovely telescope from inside of my Secret World, where I was safe to be myself.

Here, I remembered how to breathe.

I laughed heartily, like a child. I stopped walking slowly, and I started joyfully skipping over the bridge, while humming softly like a baby nightingale under my breath.

Here, I forgot how to cry.

I blessed the past and let him go. In that final act of grace, I freed *myself* from my own captivity. Soon, I found serenity in the *present* and created the *future* with true purpose and love.

The last wound was finally healed. I vowed to embrace **The One** again. It was time.

I had arrived.

To be continued in…

The One